FINDING LEAH'S LIGHT

A Firefly's Adventure

by Scott Collins

Dedicated to my Awesome Grandkids!

FREE GIFT for Book Owners!

Go to this website to claim yours:

www.FindingLeahsLight.com

Scott Collins
@ ESG Books
818 Wind Mill Lane
Kaysville, Utah 84037

Leah is a firefly.

She lives deep in the forest with her family.

They are called fireflies because they all have chemicals inside their bodies that make them glow in the dark like a lightbulb blinking on and off. It is not really fire that lights them up but they are still called fireflies, or sometimes called lightning bugs.

Every night each member of her family, and all her friends, fly around the forest blinking their lights.

That is—everyone except Leah.

Leah does not have her light.

Every night she goes out with her friends and tries, and tries, and tries to find her light.

But Leah has no light.

Leah's mother tells Leah to be patient and she will find her light when the time is right. But Leah is tired of waiting. She is tired of being the only firefly in the forest with no light.

So Leah decides she is going to search until she finds her light. She packs a lunch and sets out on her adventure early one morning.

Leah first visits some of her glowworm cousins. Glowworms make light in the same way that fireflies make light. They use chemicals inside their bodies to produce light in a process called bioluminescence. Leah hopes they might know where she can find her firefly light.

“I am looking for my firefly light. Do you know where I might find my missing light?” she asked the glowworms.

“We don’t know where you can find your light. We are still just babies,” said the glowworms, “and we don’t even know yet why we have our own lights. Sorry, we can’t help you.”

Leah politely thanked the glowworms and flew away continuing her adventure and searching for her light.

Her next stop is at the fire ant city. Leah thinks that fire ants may know something about light and fire—after all, they must be called fire ants for a reason. And she had heard that she might have some distant relatives in this fire ant city.

"I am looking for my firefly light," she explained. "Do you know where I might find my missing light?"

"We're sorry," replied the fire ants. "We don't know anything about firefly lights. We are fire ants and we get our name because of our red color and our painful sting—a sting that hurts like fire burning on the skin. Sorry, we can't help you."

Leah politely thanked the fire ants and flew away continuing her adventure and searching for her light.

As she flew away, she saw a group of ladybugs resting in the sun on some large, lush forest leaves. Leah flew over to the ladybugs.

“I am looking for my firefly light,” she explained. “Do you know where I might find my missing light?”

“We’re sorry,” replied the ladybugs. “We don’t know anything about firefly lights. Sorry, we can’t help. But if you see any aphid bugs on your journey, please let us know. We love to eat aphids and its almost lunchtime.”

Leah politely thanked the ladybugs and flew away continuing her adventure and searching for her light.

It was getting close to lunchtime so Leah landed in a nearby tree next to a large cicada bug.

"What's a firefly like you doing out during the middle of the day today?" asked the cicada bug.

Leah explained that she is searching for her firefly light. "I am the only firefly in the forest without my own light," she said sadly. "No one in my family, and no firefly in the forest, can tell me where to find my light. So today I decided to look for it myself. So far I have asked the glowworms, the fire ants, and even the ladybugs if they could help me find my light. No one has been able to help me yet."

As Leah ate her lunch, the cicada bug spoke. "I wish I could help you," he said. "But I really don't know much about firefly lights. In fact, I just spent the last 17 years underground and only emerged yesterday. But I can sing louder than most any other insect."

"If you plug your ears so they don't get damaged, I will sing out loud and see if I can call my new friend the dragonfly. We met yesterday and he is pretty smart about most everything. Maybe he can help."

Leah finished her lunch and plugged her ears. The cicada bug started singing loudly for the dragonfly. Leah was astonished at just how loud the cicada could sing. Wow! She was sure glad he warned her to cover her ears.

Leah saw the dragonfly and she flew over to meet him. "I am looking for my firefly light," she explained. "Do you know where I might find my missing light?"

"I'm sorry," replied the dragonfly. "I get around a lot and see most everything. I have more eyes than any other insect and can even see behind me. Unfortunately, I don't know anything about firefly lights. Sorry, I can't help you. But I do know where you can find the Termite Queen."

Leah politely thanked the dragonfly and flew away looking for the Termite Queen.

Why would Leah want to see the Termite Queen, you ask?

Well, the Termite Queen lives longer than most any other insect and can live up to 25 to 50 years in the right conditions. She has thousands and thousands of workers and attending termites in her nest. Because she has lived so long, and has so many workers bringing her information, she knows a lot about the forest.

Leah finds the Termite Queen after following the directions from the dragonfly.

"Oh great Termite Queen, I am looking for my firefly light," Leah explained. "Do you know where I might find my missing light?"

The old and wise Termite Queen replied simply, "Listen to your mother Leah. Mother knows best."

Leah was disappointed. She still had not found her light and it was getting dark. So Leah headed home.

Leah’s mother was excited to see her.

"Leah!" she exclaimed. "We have some new neighbors that moved in today while you were gone."

"So," moaned Leah.

"So," Leah's mother responded with excitement in her voice. "They have a very handsome boy named Luke. I told their family all about you and even showed them your picture. Now Luke is very excited to meet you."

"Mom, I don't even have my own light yet. I can't meet him," complained Leah.

Leah's mom smiled and calmly replied, "He is coming after dinner tonight to take you out flying."

Leah didn't eat much dinner. Maybe she was just anxious about meeting this new "very handsome" neighborhood firefly boy.

When the doorbell rang, Leah opened the door to find Luke standing there.

"Oh my gosh," Leah told herself, gasping out loud. Her mom was right. Luke was "very handsome!" She was so embarrassed that she began to feel warm all over.

Luke asked, "Leah, are you ready to fly?"

Leah started to reply, "Yes, but you should know that I don't have my………."

"By the way," Luke interrupted, "your light is very beautiful too, almost as pretty as you are!"

Leah looked down and was surprised! She now had her very own light. And, yes, it was bright and beautiful!

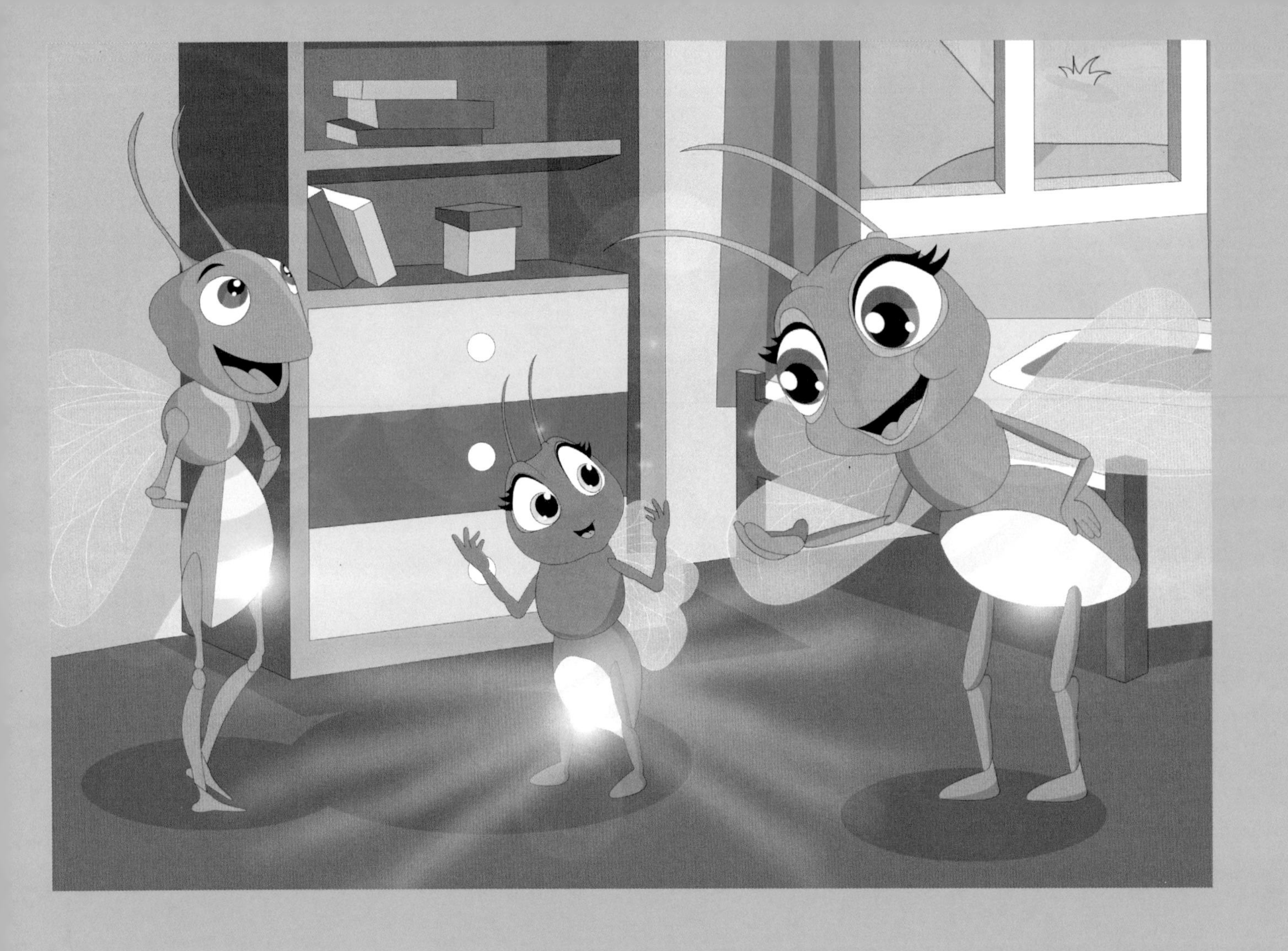

"Mom!" she exclaimed in excitement.

Leah's mom simply replied, "I see you found your light. The time must be right."

Leah and Luke flew off into the night both blinking their lights like two fireflies have never blinked before.

The End

Okay, now you've read the story. Let's see just how much you learned. Ready? Good Luck!

Question #1: What is "bioluminescence"?

1. The science of living things.
2. An ice cream flavor.
3. The chemical process that produces a firefly's light.

Question #2: Fire ants get their name because...

1. They are colored red like fire.
2. Their sting causes pain that burns like fire.
3. They build fires to keep warm.

Question #3: Ladybugs love to eat...

1. Peanut butter and jelly sandwiches.
2. Aphids.
3. Tomatoes.

Question #4: Cicada bugs live underground as nymphs (young bugs or baby bugs) before emerging as adults. How long do they live underground?

1. 17 years.
2. 17 months.
3. 17 days.

Question #5: Just how loud is a cicada bug's song? Have you heard one?

1. As loud as a library whisper.
2. As loud as a jackhammer 50 feet away.
3. As loud as a jet flyover at 1,000 feet, or a thunder clap.

Question #6: What insect has the most eyes?

1. A fly.
2. A worm.
3. A dragonfly.

Question #7: How long can a termite queen live?

1. Until she dies.
2. 5 years.
3. 25 to 50 years.

Question #8: Do mothers know best?

(Answers on next page—don't peek before answering all the questions...)

Answers

Question #1:

1. Incorrect, although "bio" means life or living things. Try again.
2. Whoops, not correct. Wow, you must be hungry. Is ice cream your favorite treat? Vanilla is my favorite—especially when I add a banana and some Oreos.
3. Yeah! You chose wisely. Bioluminescence is the production and emission of light by a living organism. It is the process by which fireflies and glow worms produce their light.

Question #2:

1. Oops, choose another answer.
2. Whoa! How smart you are! You were paying close attention in the story.
3. No, they are not like boy scouts on a cold winter night…

Question #3:

1. You might like PB&J sandwiches, but ladybugs do not. Sorry.
2. Yes, you are right! Ladybugs love to eat aphids which are little bugs that are among the most destructive garden bugs in the world. That is why gardeners love to see lots of ladybugs in their gardens.
3. Sorry, but let's put lots of tomatoes on our pizza and in our salads. They are so good!

Question #4:

1. Correct! Wow, can you imagine spending 17 whole years underground? That's what Cicada Bugs do before they become adults.
2. 17 months is almost a year and a half. It is a long time, but not long enough for cicada bugs to mature. Try again.
3. Hardly enough time to even think about the future. Guess again.

(Answers continued on next page)

Answers continued from previous page

Question #5:

1. Much louder. Try again.
2. Even louder. One more try.
3. Yep, you got it! A cicada bug can "sing" so loud that it is among the loudest of all insect produced sounds.

Question #6:

1. Sorry. Houseflies have about 6,000 eye facets that give them a panoramic view of their surroundings. But they don't have nearly as many as dragonflies.
2. Whoops. Worms don't have eyes. They only have light and touch sensitive organs. Try another answer.
3. What a good reader you are! This is the correct answer. Dragonflies have the most eyes of any insect, about 30,000 of them. Wow! And they can see in 360 degrees. Can you imagine being able to see behind yourself?

Question #7:

1. Well, you are correct that she only lives until she dies but the question is asking for a time period. Try again.
2. She is just starting her long life at 5 years old. Guess much longer.
3. Can you believe it! I couldn't! Yes, a termite queen may live up to 25 to 50 years under the right conditions. And, besides living such a long time, a termite queen is capable of producing over 30,000 termite eggs PER DAY! Holy smokes....I don't even know if I could count that high in one day.

Question #8:

Well, you will have to answer this one yourself. But, in my experience, I learned a long time ago that a loving mother's counsel is worth more than you can know at your young age.

This is **THE END, THE END.**

Made in the USA
Columbia, SC
13 August 2020